RYAN HESHKA

# WELCOME TO ROBOT TOWN

Christy Ottaviano Books
Henry Holt and Company
New York

It's a new day in Robot Town and the wheels start turning!

What a busy morning!
TrafficBot helps us
cross the street.

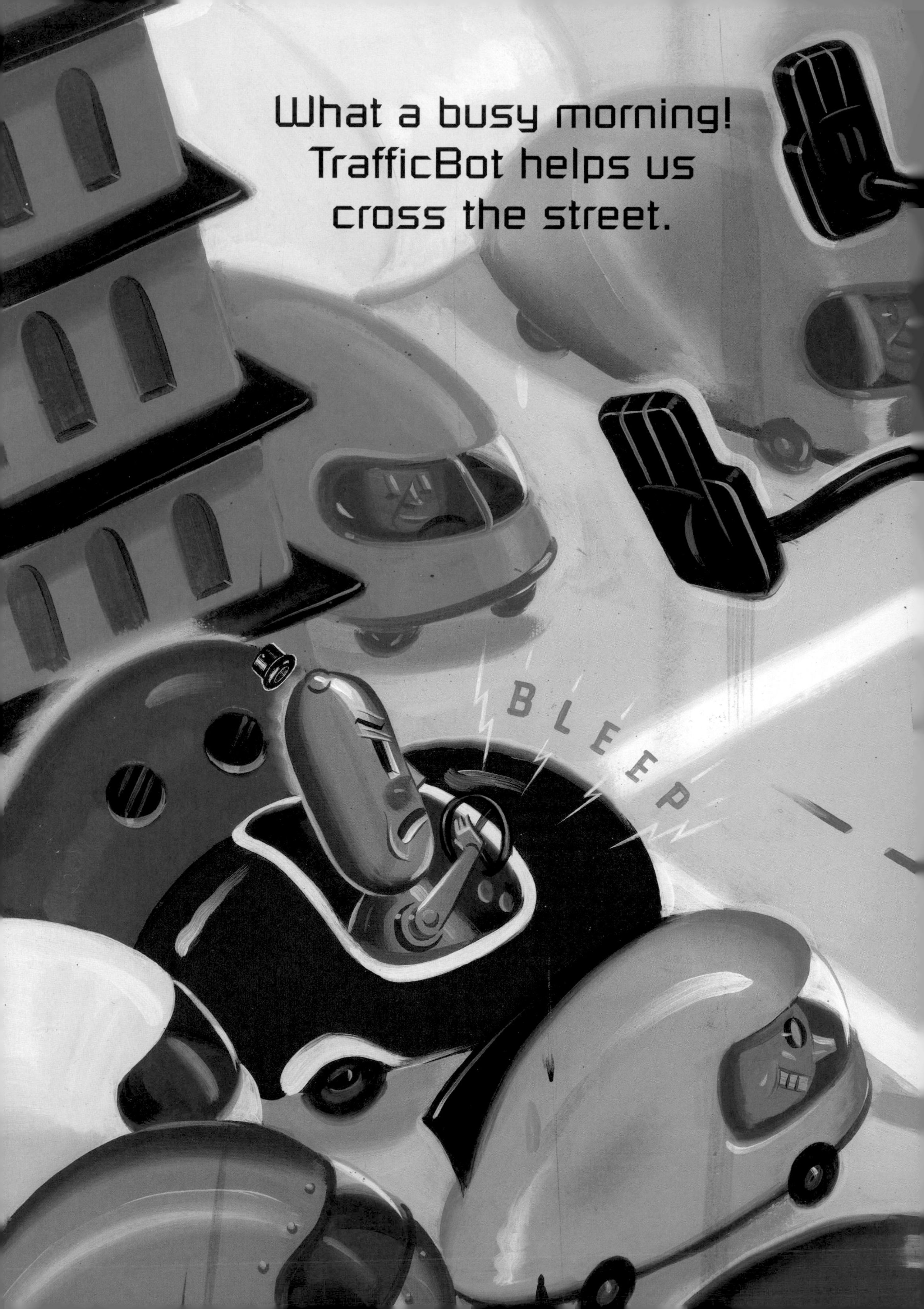

Mechanic Crank Shaft
repairs robot cars in a jiffy.

Brrrriinng! Don't be late for Robot School!

Our principal,
Professor Nutzundbolts,
is a famous inventor.

After school we head
to the playground
to burn off some energy.

There's nothing like a can
of oil to cool you off.

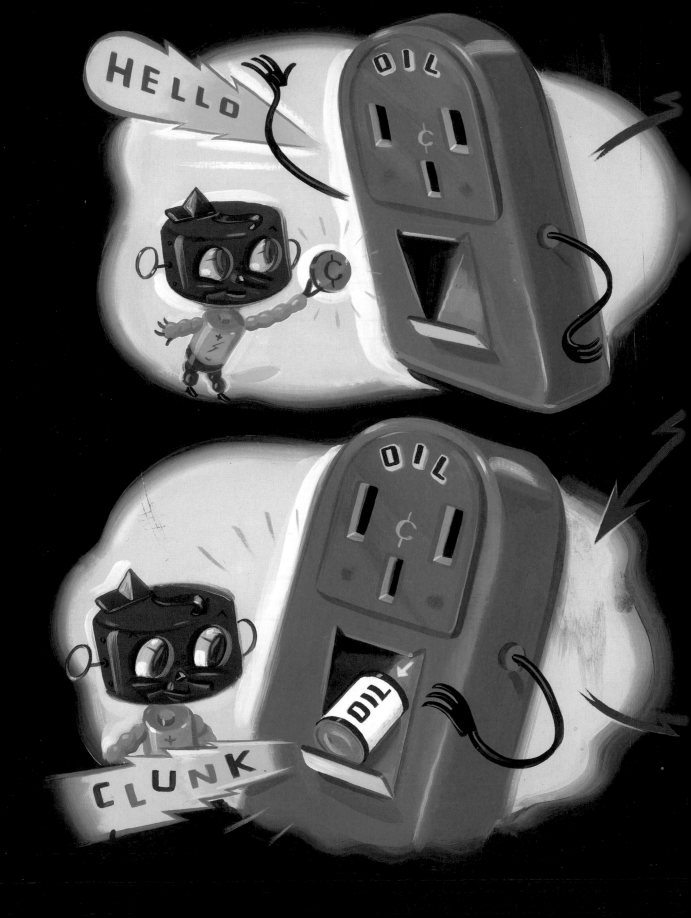

Director Steelburg
films a scary movie
on Aluminum Avenue.

If you feel under the weather,
Dr. Socket makes house calls.

The Clean-up Crew
keeps Robot Town tidy,
greased, and shiny.

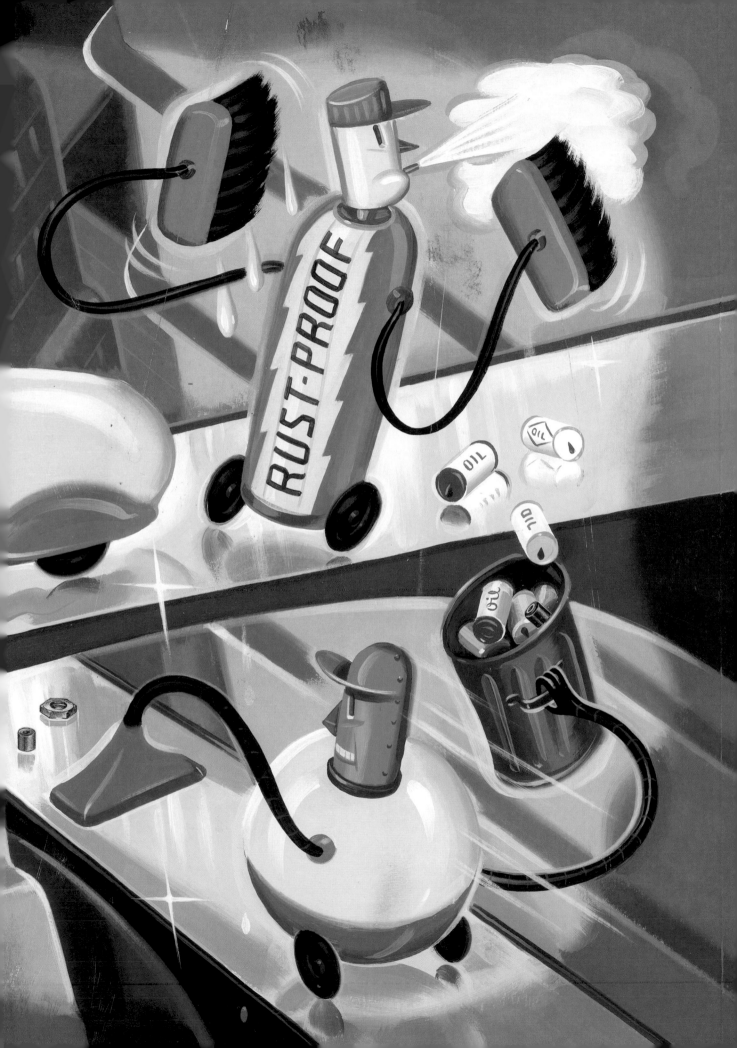

Remember, don't toss out your trash. Recyclotron can use it!

At the observatory, Telly Scope zooms in on distant planets to reveal . . .

. . . Robot Town Space Explorers in action!

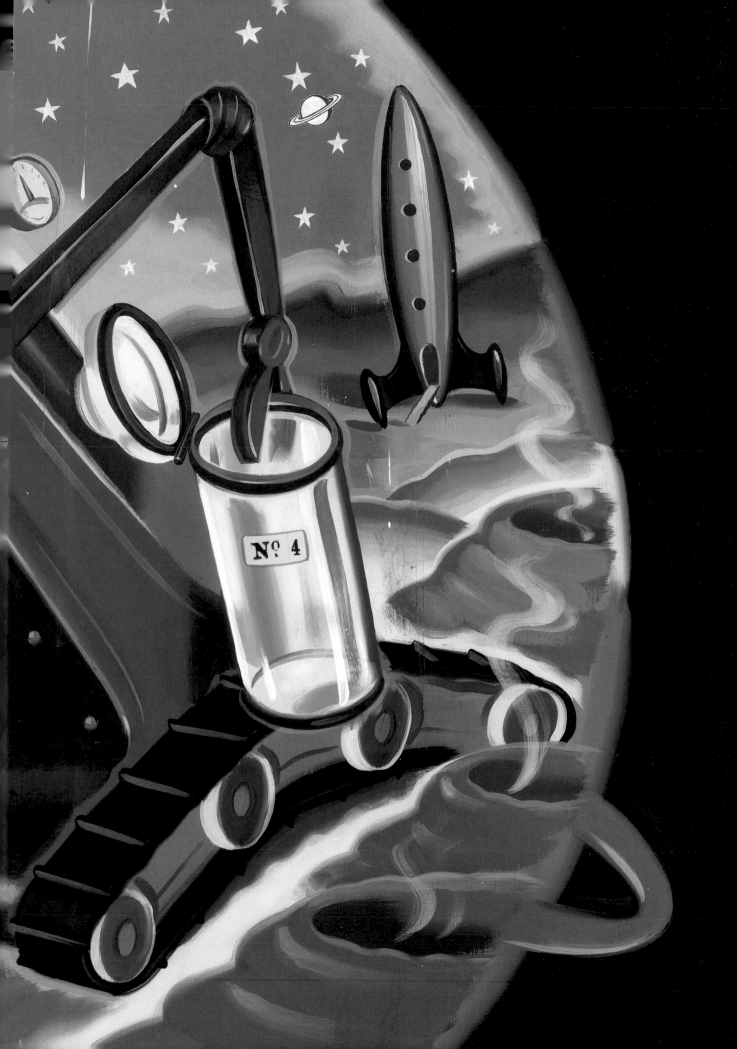

it's time to recharge and say

**GOOD NIGHT!**

## To Marinda

Thanks to Marinda Heshka, Joan, Lorne
and Tyler Heshka, Kate Larkworthy,
Monte Beauchamp (BLAB!), Kirsten
Anderson, and Christy Ottaviano

Henry Holt and Company, LLC
Publishers since 1866
175 Fifth Avenue
New York, New York 10010
mackids.com

Library of Congress Cataloging-in-Publication Data
Heshka, Ryan.
Welcome to Robot Town / Ryan Heshka. — 1st ed.
p. cm.
Summary: Simple text introduces the hardworking
residents of Robot Town, including TrafficBot and
Mechanic Crank Shaft.
ISBN 978-0-8050-8874-8 (hardcover)
[1. Robots—Fiction.] I. Title.
PZ7.H43257Wer 2013 [E]—dc23 2012021085

First Edition—2013
Acrylic and collage on
illustration board were used to create
the illustrations for this book.
Printed in China by South China Printing Co. Ltd.,
Dongguan City, Guangdong Province

1 3 5 7 9 10 8 6 4 2